The Christmas Cradle

Meadow Rue Merrill

ROSEKIDZ®

RoseKidz® is an imprint of
Rose Publishing, LLC
140 Summit Street
P.O. Box 3473
Peabody, Massachusetts 01961-3473
www.hendricksonrose.com

Book cover by Drew Krevi
Illustrations by Drew Krevi
Book layout design by Keith DeDios

ISBN: 9781628627886
RoseKidz® reorder #L50025
JUVENILE FICTION / Religious / Christian / Holidays & Celebrations
Printed in South Korea

01 5.2018.APC

To _____

From _____

Date _____

For Myla, River & Ocean
—Love, Auntie Rue

"Let your light shine so others can see it. Then they will see the good things you do. And they will bring glory to your Father who is in heaven."

Matthew 5:16

Molly pressed her nose against the front window, watching for
Aunt Jenny's truck. Tonight was Christmas Eve at Lantern Hill Farm,
and Aunt Jenny had invited Molly to help get ready for the big party.
Baby Charlie was too little to help. He didn't know about Christmas yet.
But Molly did.

Christmas was Santa and reindeer and elves!
Christmas was bright lights and a tall tree!
Best of all, Christmas was presents!

Ding-dong. Molly flung open the door for Aunt Jenny. Cousin Jacob and his little brother, Sammy, waved from the truck.

"Be a big help." Mama hugged Molly.

"Bundle up." Papa zipped her jacket.

"Gooo!" said Charlie.

"Gooo to you, too!" Molly raced out the door.

"First, we'll string popcorn," Aunt Jenny said on the way to the farm.
"Then we'll frost cookies."
Molly loved popcorn and cookies.
She loved to eat them!

But when they pulled up to the farm something was wrong.
The farmhouse door flapped open. Smoke puffed out.
"The furnace broke!" Uncle Gerry dashed toward the truck.
"The repairman doesn't know when he can fix it."
"What about the party?" asked Molly.

9

"Let's have it in the barn," said Jacob.

"But it's cold," said Sammy.

"And dirty." Molly frowned. "A barn is no place for Christmas."

"This year it will have to be." Aunt Jenny marched toward the house.

"I'll get the decorations."

Uncle Gerry filled the woodstove. Molly and Jacob swept the floor and made sawhorse tables. Sammy tied a big red bow on Marmalade, the barn cat. Two happy sheep and Briar, the donkey, peeked from their stalls.

"What about the animals?" asked Molly.

"Let's invite them to our party!" said Sammy.

"Good idea!" Aunt Jenny carried in a box of decorations.

"The first Christmas took place in a barn full of animals, too."

Maybe. But Molly was more worried about this Christmas.

Could they get ready for the party in time?

"What are you doing?" Neighbor Rosa stepped inside carrying a cake. "*Mi mita* baked *tres leches* for the party."

"Our furnace broke," said Aunt Jenny. "So we are getting ready in the barn."

"Can I help?" asked Rosa.

Aunt Jenny and Uncle Gerry strung lights. Jacob and Sammy hung sparkly stars. Molly and Rosa dressed the tables.

"What's this?" Rosa pulled a crooked cradle from the box.

15

"The Christmas cradle!" Aunt Jenny smiled.
"My grandpa helped me build it when I was your age."
"Where's the baby?" asked Molly.
"Wash up and I'll tell you," said Aunt Jenny.

Aunt Jenny told the story. "Long ago, two people set out
on a journey. The woman was expecting a baby. When they arrived at a distant village,
all the houses were full. So they slept in a barn full of animals. That night the baby was
born. He didn't have a cradle, so his mother laid him in a box of hay."
"Too bad they didn't have reindeer," said Rosa. "They could have flown in Santa's sleigh."
"And the elves could have built a cradle for the baby" laughed Jacob.
"There weren't any sleighs or elves in this story." Aunt Jenny smiled.
"No reindeer or Santa or Christmas trees either. Can you guess the baby's name?"

"Jesus!" the children shouted.

"Right!" said Aunt Jenny. "He was a king."

"Then why wasn't he born in a castle?" asked Sammy.

"This king came to serve, not boss people around," said Aunt Jenny.

"He was God's gift of love to the world."

"Is the cradle for him?" Molly asked.

"Yes," said Aunt Jenny. "Growing up, we played a game to share God's love with others. Each December, we sang carols, delivered meals, and visited people who were lonely.

Then we wrote each act of love on a card and put it in the cradle as a gift for Jesus. "On Christmas morning, we read the cards and prayed for each person we'd served. Christmas isn't about how many gifts we get, Grandpa always said, but by how many gifts we give—especially serving others."

"Like sweeping the barn," said Jacob.

"Or decorating cookies," said Sammy.

"Or making new friends!" Molly hugged Rosa.

"Exactly!" said Aunt Jenny. "There wasn't room for Jesus on that first Christmas. But we can make room by welcoming him into our hearts. Then we can share his love with our friends and neighbors so they will know how good God is."

23

The children carried the cookies and popcorn into the barn. Then they made cards to put in the cradle.

Molly wanted to give Jesus something special.
But what?

While she was trying to decide, the first vehicle pulled up the driveway. The furnace repairman! Soon the barn filled with people.

26

"We did it!" The children cheered. "We got ready for the party in time!" Molly and Jacob welcomed guests. Sammy and Rosa passed out cards and shared about the Christmas cradle. Then Molly saw someone.

"Mama! Papa!" she squealed.
Molly's parents sat on a bale of hay with baby Charlie.
A shiny star sparkled overhead.

28

The animals looked extra happy as they gazed from their stalls. Maybe a barn *was* the best place to celebrate Christmas after all.

Christmas wasn't Santa or reindeer or elves.
It wasn't bright lights or a tall tree.
It wasn't even presents.
Christmas was a baby who shared God's love
with the world so that we could share it, too.

Molly wrote her name on a heart. Then she slipped it into the cradle. She wanted to give Jesus the best present of all—herself.

To make your own Christmas cradle, gather craft sticks, twigs, a box or oatmeal container, along with glue, construction paper, paints, and glitter. Then have fun! Trace cookie cutters onto colorful paper and cut them out to use as cards on which to write your gifts for Jesus. Then set a special time—one month, one week, or even one day—to share God's love by serving others. On Christmas morning, take turns picking a note from the cradle and praying for those you've served.

For more from Meadow Rue Merrill, including other exciting ideas for celebrating God's love, visit her page on HendricksonRose.com.

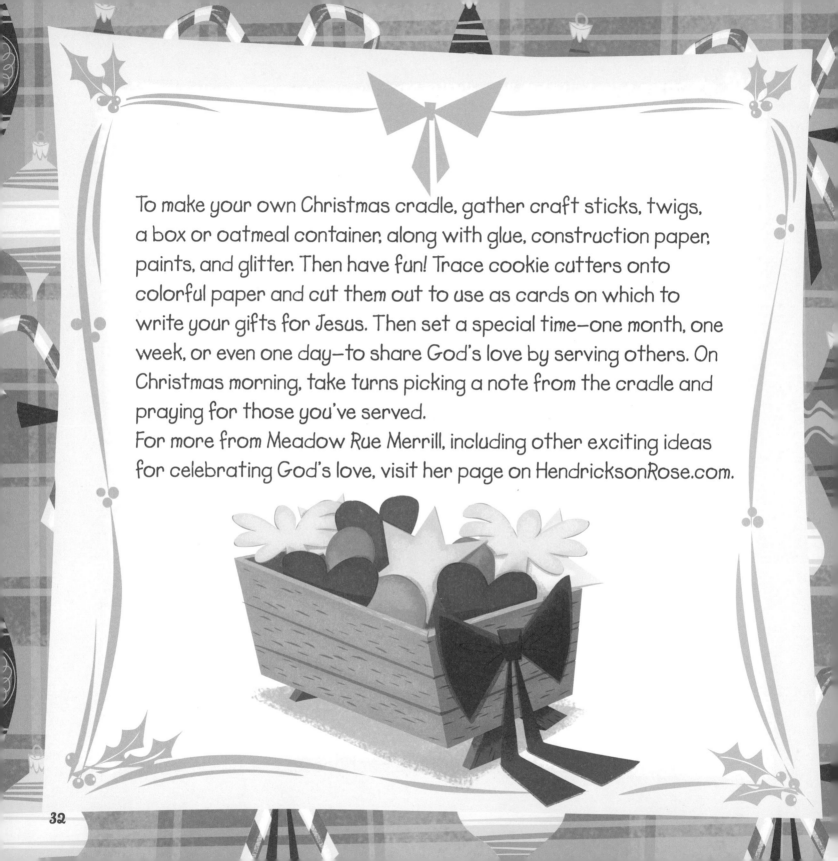